THE SURFER & THE SEAL

Printed in the United States of America

First Edition

14 13 12 11 10 / 10 9 8 7 6 5 4 3 2 1

978-0-692-44336-1

Dedicated to Logan:

*May you find the ocean
and its creatures
as magical as I do.*

Hi! My name is Paul.

I have been going to the beach since I was a little boy.
I am very lucky to live next to the ocean.

I like to go outside everyday and look at the ocean.
Sometimes I see whales and dolphins.

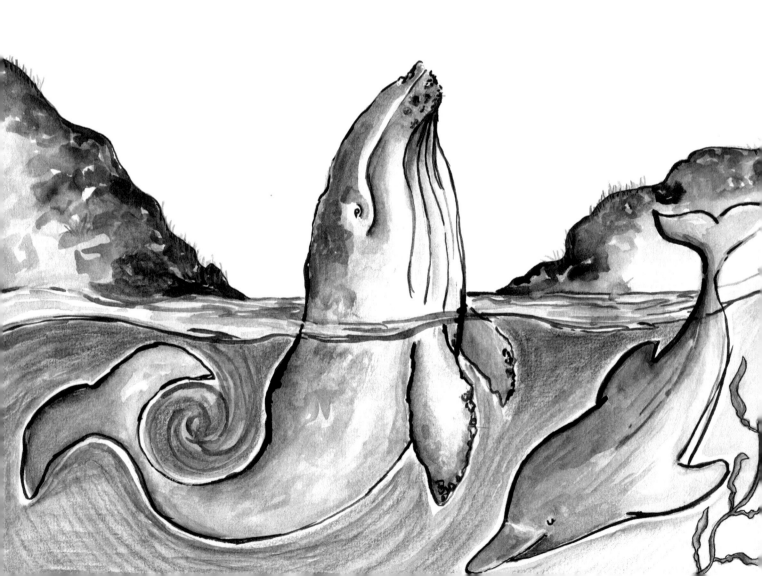

I always look for waves to see if I can go surfing.
Some days when there are good waves
I go to my secret surfing spot.

To reach my secret spot
I have to walk a long way.

Through the sand dunes, down the beach
and then along the rocky shore.

Walking along the shore, I like to stop and visit the tide pools.

I look to see if I can spot any of the special creatures who live there.

At low tide you can see many amazing animals.
There are limpets, sea urchins, octopus and crabs.

Look! There's my friend the Sea Star.

Sea Stars can live to be 80 years old
if people don't bother them.

Tide pools are magical places.

I like visiting the tide pools and saying hello to
all my friends on the way to my secret surfing spot.

Look! Here's the sea anemone waiting for something to eat.

It's been a long walk but now I'm here.
But what is that in the water?
It looks like someone is there.
I better hurry and investigate.

Hmmmm... Now I don't see anyone
but I have a funny feeling I'm not alone.

Oh my, what's that silver flash that just went under my surfboard... it's a seal and I think he wants to play!

He is very curious and wants to hang out with me.
It's a pretty big ocean so I think he
likes having a friend close by.

Now he is chasing after me
every time I ride a wave.
His head is a shiny silver so
I'm calling him Mr. Silver Head.

Every day I come out to surf, Mr. Silver Head is waiting for me. He loves to swim next to my surfboard and look up at me with his big brown eyes.

It's been a long time since I saw my friend Mr. Silver Head.
But look there's a baby seal at my secret surfing spot.
He has a silver head too and likes to swim next to me.
I think I have a new friend.

The baby seal has been surfing with me for a long time. I wonder where his mother is?

Maybe catching fish for dinner?

Wait a minute. There's Mr. Silver Head and he's feeding the baby.

Oh my goodness, Mr. Silver Head isn't a boy.
It's Ms. Silver Head and she's a mom!

Now mom and baby are both next to my surfboard and ready to play. Off we go riding waves together on a sunny day.

I'm so lucky. Now I get to surf with Ms. Silver Head and her baby. Some days they bring their friends and we all surf together.

The sun is setting after a magical day of surfing.
Time to say goodbye to mother ocean and all
my friends who live there.

I'll be back tomorrow!

About the Author:

Paul is a lover of the ocean and our natural environment. Living in Santa Cruz, California he has ample opportunity to explore nature with his dog Ella. This book is based on a true story from his surfing on the Central Coast. He is a docent at Natural Bridges State Park where he can be found leading tidepool and Monarch butterfly tours for school children. A portion of proceeds from this book will be donated to nonprofit organizations dedicated to protecting our marine resources.

About the Illustrator:

Monica is a doodler. Having graduated with a degree in molecular, cell, and developmental biology at the University of California, Santa Cruz, she aims to combine both her scientific and artistic worlds together. She is bound to get her masters in education at the San Jose State University. Above all, she loves traveling, swimming in the ocean, and cooking the best fried rice ever.

CPSIA information can be obtained
at www.ICGtesting.com
Printed in the USA
LVIC06n2303260615
444011LV00001B/1

* 9 7 8 0 6 9 2 4 4 3 3 6 1 *